*If you enjoy The Big Animal Ghost Book,*
*then you'll love these four huge collections*
*of fantastic stories:*

## The Big Magic Animal Book

The Marmalade Pony *by Linda Newbery*
Mr Wellington Boots *by Ann Ruffell*
The Wishing Horse *by Malcolm Yorke*

## The Big Book of Dragons

The Little Pet Dragon *by Philippa Gregory*
School for Dragons *by Ann Jungman*
The Bad-Tempered Dragon *by Joan Lennon*

## The Big Wicked Witch Book

Fisherwitch *by Susan Gates*
Broomstick Services *by Ann Jungman*
The Cleaning Witch *by Cecilia Lenagh*

## The Big Haunted House Book

Spooky Movie *by Claire Ronan*
Bumps in the Night *by Frank Rodgers*
Scarem's House *by Malcolm Yorke*

## The Big Bad School Book

Whizz Bang and the Crocodile Room *by Susan Gates*
A Parsnip Called Val *by Sylvia Green*
Monkey Business *by Kara May*

# The BiG Animal Ghost Book

## Ghost Dog
ELEANOR ALLEN

## Ghost Horse
ELEANOR ALLEN

## Smoke Cat
LINDA NEWBERY

Hippo

Scholastic Children's Books,
Commonwealth House, 1–19 New Oxford Street,
London WC1A 1NU, UK
a division of Scholastic Ltd
London ~ New York ~ Toronto ~ Sydney ~ Auckland

Published in this edition by Scholastic Ltd, 1999

*Ghost Dog*
First published in the UK by Scholastic Ltd, 1996
Text copyright © Eleanor Allen, 1996
Illustrations copyright © Anne Sharp, 1996

*Ghost Horse*
First published in the UK by Scholastic Ltd, 1998
Text copyright © Eleanor Allen, 1998
Illustrations copyright © Peter Kavanagh, 1998

*Smoke Cat*
First published in the UK by Scholastic Ltd, 1995
Text copyright © Linda Newbery, 1995
Illustrations copyright © Anne Sharp, 1995

Cover illustration copyright © Anne Sharp, 1999

ISBN 0 439 01140 X

Typeset by M Rules
Printed by WSOY, Finland

2 4 6 8 10 9 7 5 3 1

The rights of the authors and illustrators to be identified
respectively as author and illustrator of their work have
been asserted by them in accordance with the
Copyright, Designs and Patents Act, 1988.

# Contents

# Ghost Dog

ELEANOR ALLEN

Illustrated by Anne Sharp

*For Lucy*

# Chapter 1

Kim Martin and her mum and dad lived in a big city. Their flat was at the very top of a tall, narrow house with winding stairs. At the back of the house was a damp little yard, where the bins were kept. Along the pavement, shoppers' feet, shoppers' trolleys and shoppers' pushchairs jostled past in their hundreds, every day.

"Not a place to keep a dog," said Mum.

"Nowhere to take it walkies," nodded Dad. "It would howl with boredom. Disturb the neighbours."

"Foul the footpath," shuddered Mum.

"A £50 fine," said Dad.

"Not fair on the dog," they chorused.

"But I want a dog," said Kim. "More than anything in the world, I want a dog."

To make it up to her, they gave Kim
stuffed dogs; china dogs; wooden dogs;
mechanical dogs – every sort of dog you
can think of, that wasn't *real*. They bought
her posters of dogs for her walls and filled
her shelves with books on dogs.

"Not to worry. She'll soon grow out of it," said Mum.

"She'll have to," said Dad. "A real dog's impossible, while we're living here. . ."

But one day, the Martins' lifestyle changed. Dad got a new job. They left the cramped flat on the top floor of the tall, narrow house in the busy city. They moved to a little house that stood all alone in a big garden at the end of a lane. Beyond the garden was a field and beyond the field was a little wood. It was the perfect place for a dog.

And a dog had lived there, once.

The day they moved in, Mrs Martin complained that the house smelled of dog. She went to the supermarket for air freshener. She scrubbed and rescrubbed the floors. In the garden shed, where Dad was putting his brand-new lawnmower, he found a worn and rusty sign which said BEWARE OF THE DOG. And on the back door, Kim found old scratch marks, deeply gouged.

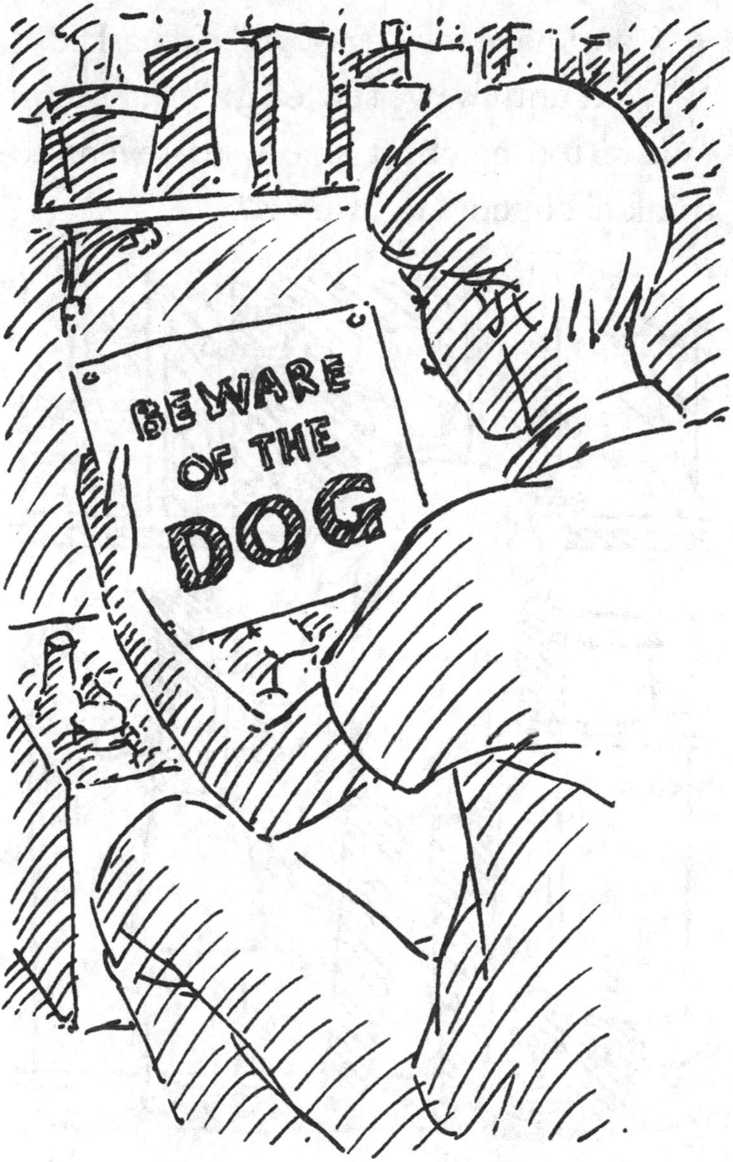
BEWARE
OF THE
DOG

"Can I have my dog now?" Kim asked.

"Wait until we've settled in," said Mum. "We're too much at sixes and sevens to think about dogs right now."

That night, as she lay in bed in her bare, new room, Kim thought she heard a dog barking and howling. It sounded close by. She climbed out of bed to investigate.

The room seemed dark without the friendly orange glow from neon street lights. And when she pulled back the curtain, the garden wasn't daytime friendly any more. It was deeply shadowy and murkily mysterious and the branches of the trees made weird and tortured shapes against the sky. From behind a cloud, the moon winked with an evil face. Instead of cheery voices and footsteps and banging car doors and roaring engines and the urgent WOW-WOW, WOW-WOW of police cars, there was no sound at all but the low, lonesome moaning of the wind in the trees.

Kim shivered. She scurried back to bed
and pulled the comforting duvet over her
head.

If only there *had* been a dog in the garden! she thought. A big, friendly dog to keep guard over them whilst they slept. . .

## Chapter 2

Next day, Kim started at her new school. It was in the village, a good mile away. Compared to her old school, it was very small. All the children seemed to know each other, like a big, close family to which she did not belong. They stared at Kim and giggled, and muttered things about her behind their hands. Kim felt more like an alien from outer space than a newcomer from the city.

"How was your new school?" Mr Martin asked, when he returned from work. Kim told him no one seemed to like her there. And it was an awful long way to walk, there and back, every day.

"Oh, dear," said Dad. "It isn't nice to feel left out. But after a while you'll be one of the gang, I'm sure you will."

"They just need time to get to know you, Kim," said Mum. "You'll soon make friends. Just wait and see."

"We could solve the other problem now, though," said Dad. "We could get her a bike to ride to school on. The roads around here are very safe."

"Good idea," nodded Mum.

"Great!" cried Kim. She cheered up quite
a bit. She had always wanted a bike, but the
roads were too dangerous in the city.

"Are *you* settling in all right?" Mr Martin asked his wife.

"Well, it's very quiet here, after the city," she said. "But I expect I'll get used to it. I can't seem to get rid of that dog smell, though. It's worst in the kitchen and the sitting room, near the hearth.

"Are we settled in enough to talk about *my* dog yet?" Kim asked. A bike was very good, but a dog would be even better. A dog that would meet her from school with a wagging tail and listen to her troubles. A dog that would be her friend.

"Don't pester," said Mum. "We've just promised you a bike. And with a dog there's a lot to think about."

"Like what?"

"Like the new carpet that's being fitted tomorrow," said Dad. "Costs a bomb. We don't want a new puppy weeing all over it."

"Or an older dog running across it with great muddy paws," added Mum.

"It could sleep in the kitchen," said Kim. "And have a kennel outside in the daytime. The back garden's perfect for a dog."

"Hmmm. That may well be," said Mum. "But who would look after it when we go back to the city to visit Grandma and Grandpa?"

"And I was thinking of putting some flower-beds out there," said Dad. "I wouldn't want them dug up. A dog needs some serious thinking about, Kim. Give us time."

Kim slammed off to her room.

Excuses, excuses!

She put up all her dog posters on the walls, unpacked the dog books, and arranged all the fluffy dogs, wooden dogs and china dogs on the bed, on the chest of drawers and on the window ledge. It looked very like the old room.

Then Kim was hit by a dreadful feeling. Supposing her parents went right on making excuses? Supposing, deep down, they didn't like dogs? Supposing they never intended to get her a real *live* dog – one that she could love and that would love her back. . .

Kim started to cry tears of loneliness and self-pity. But suddenly, the smell of dog wafted in her nostrils. Something warm and furry seemed to brush against her legs. There was nothing to be seen, but Kim's tears dried up. She felt strangely excited and comforted.

# Chapter 3

That night, Kim thought she heard the barking again. She sat up in bed and listened. This time it seemed close by, as though it was coming from the garden.

She opened the window and peered out. The air smelled country-chill and damp and full of vegetation. The lawn was a sea of silvery-grey and across it, the bushes and shrubs of the borders cast spooky black shadows. Shadows that looked like crouching, menacing dwarfs. . .

Then suddenly, one of the shadows moved.

The shadow headed stealthily towards
the garden shed. The shed where they kept
the brand-new, petrol-driven lawnmower
you could ride upon to cut the grass.
A thief!

Kim's hand flew to her mouth. Her heart thump-thumped inside her chest, and the chill of the night-time garden seeped up and shivered into her. She wanted to run to her parents' room, to shout for help, but her legs wouldn't move and fear lodged in her throat like a lump of apple.

And then another shadow moved. Crouching low, it moved menacingly across

the lawn towards the stealthy figure. And as it moved, it growled – a deep, ferocious, threatening growl. The figure stopped and jerked around. It flung up startled arms and shouted something very rude. Hands outstretched, it started gingerly to back away. Then suddenly it turned and fled. Back down the garden the thieving figure raced, and over the fence it flung itself, with the shadow dog in swift pursuit. The fencing shook as the shadow dog leapt against it, flinging back its head and firing off a string of barks that split the air like bullets.

Kim forgot her fear. She clapped her
hands in glee. "Brave dog! You saw him off!"
she shouted. "Good dog – you saved our
lawnmower! And Dad's new garden tools!"

The shadow dog threw one last bark, then trotted back across the lawn towards the house. Beneath Kim's window it stopped, sat down on its haunches, and looked up at her.

Kim could see it clearly now. It was a big dog. A very big, black dog.

She shivered with excitement.

"Do you want to come in?" she called.

The dog barked eagerly.

"Shh. . ." she said. "I'm coming down."

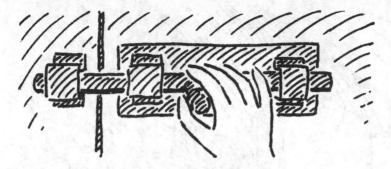

Carefully, Kim drew back the bolt on the door. A cold draught spiralled through as she opened it.

"Here, boy," she whispered, and looked out and waited.

Nothing entered.

"Here, boy," she whispered again. "Don't be shy, I won't hurt you."

She heard a whimper. But surprisingly, it came from behind her.

There, sitting by the kitchen sink, was the big, black dog. Its wide, domed head was cocked expectantly.

Kim did a double-take. "How did you get there?" she asked.

Then she shivered again and her insides screwed up like an empty crisp packet. She could see the whole sink unit, though the dog was sitting in front of it. The dog was see-through!

She stifled a scream.

The dog moved, anxiously. It sensed her alarm. Its large brown eyes stared at her pleadingly and its tail thumped gently on the floor. "Don't give me away," it seemed to be saying. "I mean you no harm."

"I'm scared of you," Kim whispered.

The dog whined softly. It raised a paw and offered it.

Despite her fear, Kim smiled. The dog seemed to smile back. Its eyes shone and its tongue lolled pinkly out of its mouth. Kim knew it was a good dog. Not a dog to be afraid of except that it was a ghost dog!

# Chapter 4

Over the next few days, Kim and the ghost dog became friends. She kept him secret from her parents. They could smell him, but they never saw him. He only appeared for Kim, when nobody else was there. He would wait by the garden gate to greet her when she rode home from school. They would go for a walk along the lane and she would tell him all her troubles.

Sometimes, as she was eating her dinner, or watching TV with her parents, she would feel his warm body brushing against her legs, or his smooth pink tongue licking her hand. It felt good to know he was still there, even when she couldn't see him.

She named her ghost dog Rex. The name came into her mind one day. And when she said it, he wagged his tail as though he knew it.

Rex was kind and as gentle as a lamb, but he was a good guard dog. Guarding the house and garden was his job. He took it very seriously. If a stranger walked along the lane, Kim would glimpse Rex, lying in wait behind the hedge, ready to bark at the first sign of trouble.

One day, Kim's mother was looking anxious. "The milkman tells me there've been some break-ins around here lately.

We ought to be more careful. Not leave doors unlocked and windows open, or the place unguarded."

Another day she said, "I was down at the bottom of the garden, weeding. I thought I heard a dog barking, inside the house. I came up the garden to investigate – and do you know what? The postman was ringing the doorbell, with a parcel. I'd have missed him, if I hadn't thought I'd heard a dog. If it had been a robber, instead of the postman, he could have stolen all we have, and I wouldn't have heard a thing."

Kim longed to tell her that the barking dog was Rex and that Rex was always on guard. But she knew Rex had to be kept a secret.

Gradually, Kim began to settle down in her new school. School didn't seem so bad, now she had her ghost dog friend at home to talk to. She looked forward to telling him all that had happened every day. Mr Martin was enjoying his new job. But Mum was feeling lonely in the new house. She missed all her neighbours in the city and she missed the noise. Now she was always worried that a thief might break into the house.

"That dog smell's still here, isn't it?" said Dad one evening.

"I don't notice it now," replied Mum. "I must have got used to it."

"I was wondering," continued Dad, "if we should think about getting that dog for Kim. It would be a friend for her and a companion for you. And I'm not getting enough exercise, now I don't play squash. It would be nice to go for a walk sometimes. But I don't like to go on my own. A dog would be a good excuse."

"I'd like a dog to guard the house and keep me company," said Mum. "The milkman tells me there's been another burglary in the village. I'd like a puppy that I could train."

"What about the new carpet?" asked Dad.

"We could keep the puppy in the kitchen until it was house-trained."

"Then it could have a kennel, outside."

"The back garden's perfect for a dog."

Kim could not believe her ears.

"We know how much you've always wanted a dog, Kim. It would be your dog," they said.

Poor Rex! Kim thought – how would he
feel? The house and garden were his. He
guarded them. What would he do if a
puppy arrived on his patch?

"But who would look after it, when we go to the city to visit Grandma and Grandpa?" she asked, in despair. "And what about the flower-beds?"

Her parents smiled. "We'll sort that out when the time comes," they said. "Just think – a dog of your very own, at last!"

Kim forced a delighted smile. She could never explain that she had a dog already. A ghost dog.

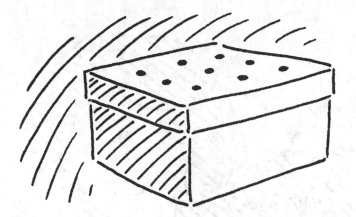

## Chapter 5

A day or two later, when Dad arrived home, he was carrying a large, cardboard box. Inside it was the wriggliest, chubbiest, most adorable puppy you could imagine.

He captured the hearts of all of them. Kim named the puppy Bobby. It seemed a round and bouncing sort of name, and this was a very round and bouncing sort of dog.

It should have been the happiest day of Kim's life. But deep inside, she felt miserable. This wasn't fair to Rex.

"I'm sorry, Rex," she muttered. "It's not my fault."

She put out her hand, but Rex didn't lick it.

She feared he was sulking.

That night, Kim could hear the puppy whimpering in its basket in the kitchen. It was feeling lonely.

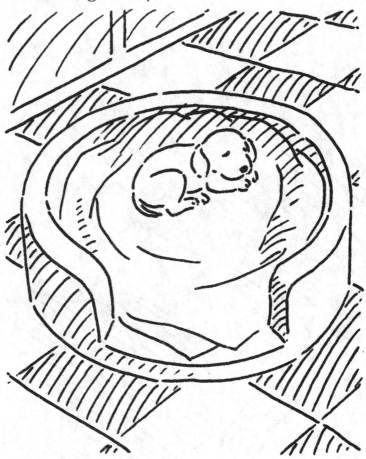

"It will whimper for a night or two," her
mum had warned. "Missing its brothers
and sisters and its mum."

But suddenly the whimpering stopped. It stopped so suddenly, Kim felt she ought to check.

She pushed open the kitchen door and peered towards the basket. The basket was overflowing with dog. In it lay Rex, or rather the half of him that would fit in it. And snuggled up against him, snoring peacefully, was Bobby.

"You've befriended him," Kim whispered.
"What a good dog you are, Rex."

Though Mr and Mrs Martin never knew it,
Rex took over Bobby's upbringing. He
taught him how to sit and stay and how to
walk to heel. He removed him from the
best armchair and stopped him digging up
the flower-beds. Most important of all, he
taught him how to be on guard.

"What an intelligent little chap Bobby is!" Mrs Martin would exclaim. "No sooner have I explained things than he seems to understand. Never once has he weed on the new carpet. And no stranger ever gets beyond the garden gate without a warning bark."

"You must be a very good trainer," said Mr Martin.

Only Kim knew the truth. Bobby was not an especially intelligent puppy, nor was Mrs Martin particularly good at training him. It was Rex who deserved all the praise. With the greatest patience in the world, it was he who put the puppy through its lessons. And Mr and Mrs Martin never knew about the sock that was chewed to bits, or the mug that was shattered. Rex carried away the evidence and buried it behind the garden shed.

# Chapter 6

As the months passed by, Bobby grew and grew. He grew not only in size, but also in confidence. He was a lovable and affectionate dog, but he was becoming a little cocky.

One afternoon after school, Kim was sitting on the back lawn with her mum. Rex, invisible, was lying at Kim's feet, relaxing because it was Bobby's turn for guard duty. Suddenly there came a dreadful barking and snarling from the front garden. Rex gave a ghostly, throaty growl and leapt to his feet, quickly followed by Kim, then Mum.

"My bike!" cried Kim. "I left it just inside the gate! I meant to move it, but I forgot."

The garden gate was swinging wide.
Twenty metres or so along the lane lay
Kim's bike, abandoned. And up the lane
fled the thief, with Bobby at his heels,
throwing triumphant barks.

"What a brave and clever guard dog you are!" cried Mrs Martin, when Bobby trotted back.

Kim felt very proud of Bobby, and so did Rex. Rex had taught him so well, he had proved he could now take charge all on his own.

Mr Martin took the old BEWARE OF THE DOG sign from the shed. He cleaned it up. And watched by Kim and Bobby and Rex he proudly nailed it back in place.

That night, Kim heard Rex barking beneath her bedroom window. She opened the window and called to him. He was sitting on the lawn, looking up at her, just like the first night they had met. But this time, Kim knew he wasn't asking to come in. Rex had come to say goodbye.

He barked three times – short, sharp barks. Then he faded back into the shadows.

Kim knew that she would never see him again. He wasn't needed any more. The house and the garden he had protected so faithfully could now be left in the capable paws of his successor, Bobby.

Kim understood. She knew Rex was happy to go. And she had her real, live dog at last – one she loved and who loved her back.

But a tear ran sadly down her cheek. She knew she would never forget the big, black friendly ghost dog she had known as Rex.

The End

# Ghost Horse

ELEANOR ALLEN

Illustrated by Peter Kavanagh

*For Barbara and Peter*

# Chapter 1

"Would you like to go riding in the summer holidays?" asked Shona's mum. "I've booked a cottage on a beautiful moor called Exmoor. It's the perfect place for riding."

"No," said Shona glumly. "You know I hate horses."

"Still?" sighed her mum.

"Yes," said Shona. "And I always shall."

When the time for their holiday came round, Shona and her mum and dad drove across the wide, open spaces of Exmoor, until they reached a large and pretty village near the sea. Their car drew up outside a white-painted cottage with black window frames and tiny panes of old glass. Hanging low over the bedroom windows was a thick, thatched roof.

Shona liked the look of their holiday cottage, but her mum had doubts.

"It's built straight on to the main street," she frowned. "I hope it won't be noisy."

"The brochure said it used to be an old coaching inn. So it would be on the main street, wouldn't it?" Dad pointed out.

"Why are there three stone steps standing in the road and going nowhere?" asked Shona.

"That's an old mounting block," said Mum. "Left over from when this was an inn. Travellers stood on top to mount their horses."

"Wonder what else is left over from the old inn days?" grinned Dad. "I could fancy a pint of beer."

Inside, there were a few low oak beams and some rather uneven floors, to remind them that this was once the Old Bull Inn. But no roaring log fires, four-poster beds and rush-strewn floors. Just a gas fire, a fitted carpet and a modern kitchen. It was clean and comfortable, but Shona felt disappointed by the inside.

Dad said some of the old stabling was still there, round the back. He had put the car in it because it was now a garage.

"Thinking of stabling," said Shona's mum, "I noticed several farms near here have ponies and horses for hire. Wouldn't it be wonderful to ride over the moor tomorrow? Have you changed your mind about riding, Shona?"

"No," said Shona firmly. "I haven't. And I never shall. I've told you already – I *hate* horses. I'll *walk* over the moor."

## Chapter 2

Once upon a time, Shona had loved horses. More than that – she had been mad about them. She'd had a few riding lessons and had been getting on just fine.

Then a friend from school called Sarah had got a pony of her own. She had invited Shona over to ride him.

Sarah's pony was a cocky little chap

called Taffy and he lived in a field behind Sarah's house. Everybody said Taffy was as good as gold. Safe as houses. And so he was. Apart from one very big flaw. And in all the excitement over showing him off, nobody remembered to warn Shona before she mounted him.

*Flop*, *flap*, *flop*, went Shona's waterproof jacket as the wind caught it.

Taffy pricked up his ears. What strange noise was that, on his back? He didn't like it.

Taffy knew he more than didn't like it – he was scared of it. More than scared – terrified! He wanted to get away from it. He panicked. He kicked up his heels and bolted away down the field. Shocked out of her wits, Shona screamed and clung on tight.

Sarah, her big brother Tom and her mum were in the field. But there was nothing they could do.

For a second or two, Shona was so busy screaming and trying not to fall off, she didn't notice where they were heading –

straight for a prickly hawthorn hedge.
When she did see it, she panicked too!
She was about to fling herself off. But at
that moment, Taffy thought of a different
way to rid himself of the scary noise.

He bucked and shot Shona off.

The ground seemed to rise up and hit Shona like a great iron fist. She lay bruised and shaken and very, very shocked. As she gazed up at the high, prickly hawthorn hedge, she shuddered. She had almost landed in that!

Sarah, with her brother and mum, ran to pick her up and check for broken bones. They were relieved she seemed okay. They caught Taffy and calmed him down, then explained to her what had happened.

"You should take your jacket off and get back up," they urged. "You have to get your confidence back. Up you get."

White-faced and tense, Shona refused. She didn't want to get back up – not on Taffy, not on any horse. Ever again.

Horses weren't fun to Shona any more. They did strange things she couldn't control. Horses were dangerous, unpredictable creatures – creatures to fear.

# Chapter 3

A wind from the sea was sweeping over the moor that afternoon. It was a feather ruffling, boat-buffeting wind with an icy sharp edge to it, like the cut of waves. It lifted Shona's hair and plucked at her skirt as she ran across the cobbled yard behind the Old Bull Inn towards the garage. She had left her book in the car.

The garage was a sheltered spot. It

smelled faintly of petrol and cooling-down metal. Shona took her mum's keys from her pocket and unlocked the car. She took her book from the back seat and locked up again carefully.

The warmth of the garage seemed welcoming. Shona looked around. It was built of old blocks of orangey-pink and grey-green stone. Set high up was a round-shaped window, edged with brick. Sunshine was streaming through the window, bathing the far end of the building in a golden light. That end was piled with junk – broken furniture, rusting tools and empty paint tins. And there was an old wooden partition of some sort too. Shona felt curious to know what was behind it.

It was an empty stall. The only one

still left from the days when this had been stabling for the busy coaching inn.

Shona sniffed and her face turned pale. Horse!

Shona sniffed again. The smell was stronger now, and getting stronger all the time. Warm and strong, it overpowered the smell of car.

The rays of sun dazzled her eyes.

Shona put up a hand to shade them.
She blinked. And when she looked
again into the empty stall, it wasn't
empty any more.

A horse was standing there.

Shona screamed. It was a piercing,

blood-curdling scream inside her. But what came out was shrivelled and shrunken. More like a gasp.

Shona's hand gripped the side of the stall. Her brain told her to run away, but her body wouldn't move.

It was no more than a shadow horse at first. But before her eyes, it began to flesh out, into a solid horse. Not a horse for pulling coaches. Not an ordinary horse – a magnificent horse.

It was a stallion, the colour of polished steel, with a mane and tail like pure white, silken thread. A horse so beautiful, it took Shona's breath away.

Though she still trembled from head to toe, a feeling of delight and wonderment crept over her. She stared at the horse as if bound by a spell.

The horse stirred; it stamped a hoof and flicked its ears. It knew that she was there.

Then Shona gasped in pity and surprise. For on the horse's legs she saw some nasty cuts. Another wound was bleeding on its flank and its neck had been grazed by a rope.

"What happened to you?" she whispered.

The horse turned its head towards her. Its eyes were gentle and intelligent. It seemed to know she felt sorry for it.

Shona cautiously drew a little nearer. Though she felt sorry for the horse and fascinated by it, she was still afraid of it.

The beautiful creature whinnied softly. "Help me," its soft brown eyes seemed to say. "Please help me," they pleaded.

Shona's knees felt trembly. She shook her head unhappily. "Why are you asking me? I'm scared of horses. I can't help you."

"I know you're afraid," the horse's eyes seemed to say. "But you must overcome your fear. Then you can help me."

"How can I help you?" Shona asked nervously.

"Come nearer, don't be scared. Come closer," urged the horse. "Touch me, touch me. . . ."

Shona drew a little nearer. She put
out a trembling hand. It hovered
fearfully over the horse's flank. She felt
his warmth. She almost touched. . .

"Shona! Shona! We're going out to
eat!"

Her mother's voice rang out across
the yard. A shrill voice from the human
world. And the warm horse flesh began
to fade away.

"Oh, don't go," Shona whispered.
"Please don't go. . .!"

But the horse had already gone. Her mum had scared it away.

Shona didn't tell Mum about the horse. She knew it was a secret between the two of them.

She wondered how the poor, beautiful creature had been injured. And if she would ever see it again.

And why it was a ghost horse, needing her help.

THE HIGHWAYMAN

## Chapter 4

That evening, Shona and her mum and dad went to eat in the family room of the pub down the road.

"Nice pub," said Shona's mum, as they studied the menu. "I wonder if the Old Bull used to look like this in the past?"

"Staying at the Old Bull Inn, are you?" asked the friendly landlord. He leaned across the bar and winked at

Shona. "Has links with a famous highwayman, that place, m'dear. Had you heard?"

Shona shook her head.

"How about that!" said Dad. "What was his name?"

"His name was Captain Trevelyan."

Shona looked at the landlord sharply.

A strange feeling had passed over her when he said that name.

"Did he have a horse?" she asked.

"Course he did. How could he be a highwayman, without a horse?"

Shona swallowed.

"What was his horse called?" she asked.

"His horse was as famous as he was," said the landlord. "Its name was Whistlejacket."

Shona's heart leapt with excitement. She pictured the magnificent ghostly stallion in the stable. Whistlejacket! A name to suit a horse like that, with a coat like polished steel. She pictured him galloping over the moor, as fast as the wind; as fast as a bullet fired from a pistol.

"Whistlejacket. . ." she murmured dreamily.

"There's a story about the two of them," said the landlord. "Want to hear it?"

Shona shivered with excitement. "Yes, please," she said.

"Well, one night, it's said that soldiers lay in wait for Captain Trevelyan at the Old Bull Inn. They planned to capture him and see him hanged.

"They heard the clip-clop of Whistlejacket's hooves down the dark, cobbled street and cocked their muskets.

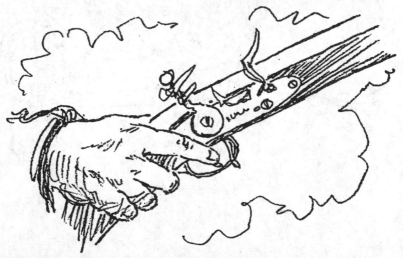

Then the horse came into view and – he
was riderless!"

"Where was Captain Trevelyan?"
"Nobody knew. Had he been tipped
off about the trap? Had he suffered an
accident – or what?

"Anyway, they had the horse. They cornered it in the inn yard. They tied it into a stall with the stoutest rope they could find, and barred it in with the stoutest bars."

"Poor Whistlejacket!"

"Captain Trevelyan loved that horse. There was no way he'd be separated from it, alive or dead. So they waited for him to appear. They say the horse was there for days, and it would neither eat nor drink. But Captain Trevelyan never showed up. From time to time, though, a low whistle could be heard, like the master was calling him. And when the horse heard that whistle, he went mad! He crashed his hooves against the stall and fought like a fury to free himself. But they'd tied him up so tight, and barred him in so well, he couldn't get out.

"And then, one morning, they found he'd stopped his struggling. He'd given up and breathed his last."

"Ugh!" said Mum. "That's not a very nice tale! And then, I suppose, they captured Captain Trevelyan and hanged him?"

"Nobody knows what happened to Captain Trevelyan. They say he was never seen again."

"Hey, come on, Shona – eat up!" urged Dad. "I thought you were hungry."

"It's the landlord's fault," muttered Mum. "Filling her head with scary tales about highwaymen. She'll be having nightmares next."

"Don't worry about it, Shona," said her dad. "It's only an old story. They probably made it up for the tourists. I bet Captain Trevelyan never really existed."

"Whistlejacket did," said Shona softly to herself. "Poor Whistlejacket did."

Her lips trembled. She was trying not to cry.

# Chapter 5

That night, Shona woke up suddenly. The bedroom was dark; it was just after midnight. Something had woken her. She listened hard. A sound came, faint but shrill. It sounded like a whistle.

And then she heard another noise. It was the whinny of a horse. Again the whistle came and again the whinny, answering it.

Then a crashing and a pounding started – fit to raise the dead!

"Whistlejacket!" Shona muttered and her heart went thump, thump, thump. "The ghost of Captain Trevelyan is whistling for him, like the landlord said, and he's trying to escape!"

In a panic, she climbed out of bed and headed for the safety of her parents'

room. They were fast asleep. Through all that noise! She wondered whether to wake them. No. Whistlejacket had faded away at the sound of her mother's voice that afternoon. He had chosen to appear only to her. So perhaps she was the only one who could hear him now?

Whistlejacket whinnied again. An urgent call. A call that seemed to be for *her*.

"He wants me to help him escape!" gasped Shona. "That's what he wants!"

Shona shrank back against the landing wall. Her heart went out to the poor, trapped creature, but she was shaking with fear.

How could a girl who was afraid of horses help a magnificent, ghostly stallion in a frenzy to escape from his stall in the middle of the night?

And what about Captain Trevelyan? He had whistled, so his ghost must be out there somewhere, prowling around in the dark.

Again the stallion called to Shona. Again he pounded at his stall.

"Why have you chosen me?" she wailed.

She covered her ears, but the pleading call echoed inside her head. She knew she would never be able to forget that call. Or to forgive herself, if she let him down. If she did nothing at all to help. She *had* to conquer her fear.

One, two, *three*! She drew a deep
breath and plunged towards the moonlit
stairs, raced down and let herself out
into the yard. The chilly night air struck
through her pyjamas and the mossy
cobblestones felt cold and damp
beneath her feet.

She tried not to look at the shadows lurking on the edges of the yard as she ran across.

She creaked open the stable door. It was warm inside and reeked of horse. A dim light shone from an old-fashioned lantern, close to Whistlejacket's stall.

Shona saw him. He was rearing and tugging and straining at the rough rope halter; he was throwing and cutting himself against the sides of the stall and pounding at the planks of wood with his hooves. The air was full of flying strands of straw and dust.

Shona cowered back and stared. She felt so small and useless. But she felt full of pity, too.

Out of pity she murmured, "Calm down, Whistlejacket. Calm down. Please don't hurt yourself any more. Please!"

The stallion heard her voice and pricked his ears. His eyes still rolled wildly and his flanks heaved and shook. But his rearing and pounding stopped. He went very still, waiting. Waiting for her to draw near.

The scary smell of horse was overpowering. And though he was very still, Shona feared Whistlejacket's tremendous power, which she knew she couldn't control.

But he was injured and a prisoner. If only she could conquer her fear of him, Whistlejacket could be free.

Shona forced herself forward. She tugged and heaved at the stout bars across the stall until she managed to move them. That gave her confidence. Gathering up all her courage, she stepped into the stall.

Whistlejacket stood so still and calm, he scarcely seemed to breathe.

Shona eyed the halter and gasped in despair. The horse's straining, tossing head had tightened the simple knots in the stout, old rope. She feared her trembling hands could never undo them. But at that moment, Whistlejacket

gently lowered his head, lessening the strain on the rope. The knots slackened just enough for Shona's nimble fingers to work on them, tugging and pulling until, at last, she had done it – she had set him free!

Whistlejacket tossed and shook his head in excitement and delight – free at last of that dreadful rope. And Shona felt so full of relief and happiness for him, she wanted to clap and cheer.

Then gently, Whistlejacket bent and nuzzled her hand in gratitude. Shona timidly stroked his muzzle, and suddenly, in a rush of warmth, she put her arms around his neck and hugged him and realized that her fear had gone. Whistlejacket had helped her to conquer her fear. They had helped each other.

And then the whistle came again.

Whistlejacket pricked up his ears and snorted. Then he backed gently out of the stall. With a soft whinny of farewell, he trotted off into the dark, starry night to join his master.

Shona ran after him to the stable door. "Goodbye, Whistlejacket!" she cried.

Across the yard, Whistlejacket turned. Upon his back now gleamed an old-fashioned saddle. And in the saddle was a shadowy figure. A figure that waved a friendly arm to Shona, as though in thanks.

With a plunge of hooves, Whistlejacket and his rider leapt into the shadows and were gone. After more than two hundred years, the highwayman and his horse were together again.

Shona ran shivering back across the quiet yard. She didn't feel afraid of the shadows any more.

As she lay in bed, she pictured Whistlejacket with Captain Trevelyan on his back, galloping joyfully over the rolling moorland, his mane and tail flying in the wind. Free.

She felt happy for them. But, deep down, she couldn't help feeling sad for herself, and a little envious of Captain Trevelyan.

The ghost horse had conquered her fear and she had set him free. But now she would never be able to see or touch the beautiful creature again. She longed to see him, just one more time.

# Chapter 6

Next day, Shona and her parents went to the seaside. Afterwards, they drove back across the moor. From time to time Shona caught glimpses of the wild ponies that lived there. And other horses with riders on their backs, hired out from local farms. Her eyes searched the rolling fields, the bleak, barren places and the deep green valleys, full of trees. But there was no sign of the one horse she wanted so much to see. If only she could see Whistlejacket, just one more time. . .

That night, Shona couldn't sleep. She felt all fizzed up inside, as though something exciting was about to happen. The hands on her travel alarm clock said nearly midnight. Still she hadn't slept a wink.

Suddenly she heard a sound.

She shot up in bed and listened hard.

Clip-clop, clip-clop, clip-clop.

Next minute she was at the window.
Bursting with joy, she was leaning out
beneath the thick, sweet-smelling
thatch.

Clip-clop, clip-clop, clip-clop.

Along the street trotted Whistlejacket,
fearless and proud, his head held high.
The old-fashioned saddle was on his
back. But this time it was empty. He had
come alone.

The stallion stopped beneath her window and looked up. He called softly to her and pawed the ground. And then he stood, very still, beside the big, stone mounting block. Waiting.

"Waiting for me!" gasped Shona. "He wants me to ride him!"

She pulled a sweater and a pair of jeans over her pyjamas and thrust her feet into a pair of trainers.

She let herself out of the old front door and ran across to the mounting block. She felt no fear as she clambered into the saddle and took a firm grasp of the pommel.

Then off Whistlejacket flew up the village street, as smooth and swift as a bird, with Shona on his back.

Out of the village and into the moonlit countryside they galloped. Over an ancient, hump-backed bridge. Along a valley, its steep sides wooded with fir and beech. Branches made a dark, mysterious tunnel over their heads. And beside the narrow path, a stream sparkled and splashed and tumbled.

Then the moor. Vast and rolling, mile after mile; silver-tinted under the bright full moon. Shona felt Whistlejacket's thrill as he leapt forward, flying over the highest part of the moor – on top of the world, it seemed.

This was *really* riding! Shona thought.
This was sensational!

Down to their right sparkled an inlet
of the sea.

No sooner had Shona seen it and wished, than they were there. Galloping along the beach with the spray in their faces and the wind in their hair. Shona laughed and shouted with pleasure. On the back of the beautiful Whistlejacket she felt no hint of fear.

Back through sleeping villages and lonely valleys they flew. Back over the highest places on the moor where the whole world seemed theirs. And back at last to their own village street and the mounting block by the Old Bull Inn.

Patiently Whistlejacket waited for Shona to dismount. She gave him one last hug, and then he turned away. Sadly

Shona wiped away a tear as Whistlejacket clip-clopped away from her, back up the village street towards the moor.

As he reached the very last house, there came a ghostly whistle, thin and shrill on the still night air. Then a figure sprang from the shadows and leapt up into the saddle. It was Captain Trevelyan. The dashing highwayman turned and doffed his hat to her. A last goodbye. Then Whistlejacket reared and plunged, his hooves sending up sparks from the cobblestones, and the beautiful ghost horse and his master were gone for good. Free at last to chase the wind across the moor, for ever and ever.

# Chapter 7

Next morning, Shona awoke with a heavy sadness in her heart. As though she had awoken from a beautiful dream she would never be able to recapture.

And then she remembered how Whistlejacket and Captain Trevelyan had shown their gratitude to her by giving her that ride. Pleasure and sadness were rolled into one as Shona relived the ride that was beyond anything this world could offer.

Shona got out of bed and pulled on her sweater and jeans which were in an untidy bundle on the floor. On the front of her sweater was a hair. It was a pure white hair, as smooth as a thread of silk.

A hair from Whistlejacket's mane!

Shona looked at the hair and her sadness faded. Something of Whistlejacket remained.

She took off the silver locket she wore around her neck. She twisted the hair into a little knot and locked it safe inside. "Mum," said Shona at breakfast, "what are we doing today?"

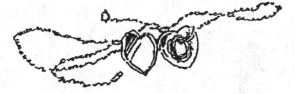

"What would you like to do?" asked Shona's mum. "Shall we take a picnic on to the moors?"

"I'd like to go riding," said Shona.

"What? Riding? You've changed your mind? I don't believe it!"

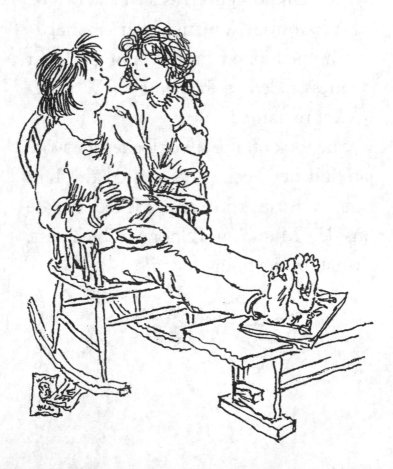

Shona's parents went riding with her. Her dad had a big bay horse called Drummond; her mum had a pretty mare called Janey. Shona herself had a small piebald pony called Aladdin.

Shona mounted Aladdin a little nervously, but with determination too.

The thrilling ride on Whistlejacket had made her determined to ride again.

Determined to become a really first-rate rider, like Captain Trevelyan.

They went for a long trek over the moor, discovering places they could never have reached on foot. It was a glorious day. The sun shone; the yellow flowers on the gorse bushes glowed; and in the

distance, the sea sparkled and danced. Shona found she was having a wonderful time. Aladdin was kind and willing and obeyed her every move – so small and controllable, after Whistlejacket! With each minute that passed, her confidence increased and her enjoyment grew.

"Shona's riding has improved no end, hasn't it?" Dad marvelled. "All her confidence has returned. In fact – I think it's doubled!"

"Like magic! agreed Mum, proudly.

Shona smiled and touched the silver locket round her neck. No magic. It was Whistlejacket who had given her back her confidence, in return for his freedom. She would never forget that.

Shona knew she would always enjoy riding from now on. She would have some wonderful rides and know some beautiful horses.

But no ride would be as special as her night-time ride across the moor.

And no horse would ever be as beautiful as the ghost horse, Whistle-jacket.

The End

# Smoke Cat

LINDA NEWBERY

Illustrated by Anne Sharp

*For Kate, Jonathan and Alexander*

## Chapter 1

As soon as they saw 16 Parkside Terrace, Simon's mum and dad decided that this was the house for them.

"I've always wanted to live in an old house," Dad said. "A house other people have lived in. It's like an old pair of shoes, creaky and comfortable."

Simon wasn't sure. He thought of the

new houses they'd been to look at, with bright clean paintwork and fresh wallpaper. He would have liked to live in one of those. But Mum said, "They've

got no personality." She and Dad had the same ideas about houses, which was just as well. And this house was quite close to their old one, so Simon wouldn't have to change schools.

Dad said, "It's going to be a home, not just a house."

So they moved into the tall thin house
that was nearly a hundred years old. It
was made of red brick and it was
sandwiched between others in a row like
soldiers standing to attention. It had
long narrow rooms with high ceilings,
and there was a long narrow garden
behind it. Simon's bedroom was at the

back. He liked the high ceiling and the old-fashioned fireplace, but he wasn't sure about all the other people who had lived there, who had slept in this room during its hundred years. He didn't know who they were, or what thoughts and memories and dreams they might have left behind.

It was the fireplaces that had really made up Mum's and Dad's minds. There were three – one in the main room downstairs, and one in each bedroom. Mum had always wanted a house with a real fireplace.

She stood in the downstairs room and said, "We can have a log fire sometimes. Won't that be lovely on a cold day?"

Simon thought it would, especially when Dad talked about roasting chestnuts in the ashes. But winter was a long way off. It was summer now, and the best thing about the house was the garden. It was much better than the bare fenced squares that went with the brand new houses, or the tidy patch they'd left behind at their council house. It was a real jungle of a garden, with tangly bits and hidden corners and shadowy secret places, and a high fence separating it from next door's garden.

Everything in the garden seemed eager to grow as big and as high and as lush as it could. The plants in the borders spilled

over on to the grass as if they had lost their balance. Ivy and honeysuckle clambered up the fence. Flowers whose names Simon didn't know stretched up their heads as if they wanted to get as near to the sun as they could. It was a garden for exploring, for crawling into the damp earthy shadowy places. There were snails and slugs and spiders and worms and ladybirds and caterpillars, and once Simon found a puff of scattered

feathers and a few small bones. There were thistles and nettles and brambles and plants with thick juicy stems, and berries that were not to be eaten. Simon knew he shouldn't eat them because they were black and glossy and delicious-looking, like poisonous berries in a fairy story.

"I shall have to do something with that garden," Mum said.

Simon wondered what she meant. The garden didn't need anything done to it. Everything in the garden knew what to do. The plants grew and the insects hatched and crawled and flew and nibbled.

Best of all, there was an apple tree. The blossom had finished and you could

already see the new little apples coming. There were helpful branches stretching out at right-angles and in just the right places, so that Simon could quite easily climb up to more than twice his own height above the ground, and wedge himself safely into a fork where the branches divided. From there, he could look down into the garden next door.

# Chapter 2

Next door's garden was just as long and narrow, but less jungly. There were flowering shrubs and bushes planted all the way along its edges and in a big flower bed that was right in the middle of the lawn, like an island. Someone looked after the garden very well, Simon could tell. An old lady was walking very slowly along the border, talking to herself At least, that's what Simon thought she was doing at first, until he realized that she was talking to the plants. He clung tightly to the apple branch and listened.

"And how are you today, William?" the old lady asked a rose bush with peachy flowers. "My goodness, you are looking glossy. You always did enjoy the sunshine. Charlotte, my dear, you must stand up for yourself more – this forsythia will take up all the space if you let her.

Gloria, how lovely to see you growing so tall and strong – you're going to be a fine lady one of these days. Frederick, you have a good rest now till next spring; you've earned it. Now, where's Blue. . ."

She was quite close to Simon. She wore a long brown cardigan and a tweedy skirt, and her grey hair was so thin that the pink of her scalp gleamed through it. She stretched out her hand to touch the leaves and petals of each plant as she spoke to it. Simon could see the papery skin of her hand, and the fingers, knobbly like twigs, and the big loose ring she wore on her left hand.

Simon thought she must be mad. He'd heard of people talking to plants – Mum did it sometimes, telling the Swiss cheese plant how clever it was to grow a new leaf, and according to the newspapers Prince Charles did it all the time. But this old lady gave them names. People's names. He was just wondering whether every plant in next-door's garden had a name, when the old lady turned round and saw him. She froze, with one hand stretched out to touch a tall white daisy in the island bed, and she stared at him.

Without meaning to let go of the branch he was clutching, Simon found himself slithering down from his perch and landing on the ground with a painful twist of his right ankle. He had grazed his hands and his knee on the apple-tree bark and he had landed hard on one elbow. He waited for a few moments,

very quietly, expecting the old lady's face to appear over the fence – she would probably tell him off for spying on her. Although he hadn't really been spying. All he had been doing was climbing a tree in his own garden.

"I don't like that lady next door," he told Mum when he went in for his tea. "She talks to herself."

Mum looked surprised. "Hazel? Oh, but she's really nice. We all talk to ourselves sometimes."

Simon wasn't sure about the old lady. He thought she might have told him off if he hadn't dropped down out of sight. She looked as if she might be strict. He didn't think Hazel was the right name for her at all. She ought to be called Mrs or Miss something.

## Chapter 3

There was an alleyway at the end of the garden, which was the way Simon came in when he got home from school each day. One afternoon he let himself in at the back door to hear voices talking in the front room – Mum's and somebody else's. He went in, hoping there might be cake, and saw a lady of Mum's age or perhaps a bit older, with curly permed hair and bright red earrings. She was holding a mug of tea and she smelled of perfume. She smiled at him and said, "Hi, Simon," as if she had known him for ages. "I'm Hazel from next door."

That explained it! Mum had got this lady mixed up with the other one. He knew the old lady couldn't be called Hazel, and he couldn't imagine this one wandering round the garden talking to the plants. She looked too energetic, as if she might jump up from her chair any minute and start playing hide-and-seek; she was a jolly-looking person, unlike the older lady, who had looked quite sad.

"Hello," he said politely, really more interested in the cake. There *was* cake, a chocolate one with flake decoration.

"Does someone else live in your house?" he asked Hazel.

She laughed, as if she thought it was a funny thing to ask. "Just Bill. My husband. Have you seen him? You can't miss him – he's a great big bloke. Rugby-playing type."

And then it occurred to Simon that perhaps Hazel lived in the house on the other side – they had two next-door neighbours, after all. Perhaps he had been the one who made the mistake, not

Mum. But when she left (after having a second piece of cake), Simon watched from the window, and saw her turn right and go up the path next door – the path to the house where the old lady lived.

"That wasn't the person I meant at all," he told Mum. "The one who was talking to herself."

Mum shrugged. "Perhaps she had someone to stay."

Simon didn't think the old lady was just staying – she had looked as if she lived there, knowing all the plants the way she did. But he didn't think about it any more that day, because he had a new computer game to play with and a drawing to do for school. He didn't think about it any more at all, until a few nights later when he woke up suddenly in the middle of the night to hear a voice calling, outside in the garden. The old lady's voice.

He couldn't hear *what* she was calling, but it went on and on, as if calling for someone who didn't come. He tried to go back to sleep, but the more he tried, the wider-awake he became. Eventually he got out of bed and pushed back the curtains.

It wasn't the middle of the night, as he had thought. It was just starting to get light; he could make out the dim shapes of trees, fences and flower-beds. And in the garden next door, the old lady, stretching out her arms and calling.

"Charlotte!" He could hear now what she was saying. "Georgina, there's a good girl. Gladys, time to rest now. Geoffrey! Here's your place. Blue! Oh, Blue, won't you come?"

She was calling to the *plants* – Simon recognized the names. It was strange enough to be standing out in the garden at about three o'clock in the morning, but odder still to be calling out to *plants*.

And even more odd besides if she didn't actually live there.

She kept bending down to touch something, and as Simon's eyes adjusted to the first grey light he could see shadows moving around at her feet, rubbing against her legs – soft, fluid, furry shadows, like cats. Although they were shadowy, Simon could make out

the different colours: black cats, white cats, tabby cats, pied cats, marmalade cats. The old lady welcomed each one, stroking it, talking to it in a soft voice, until she was surrounded by a moving carpet of purring cats, weaving, twining, arching their backs to be stroked. And every few moments she would break off to stand upright and gaze around, and she would call. "Blue! Blue, won't you come?"

189

Simon didn't actually see them do it –
one minute they were there and the next
they were gone – but the shadowy cats
seemed to melt away into the ground, or
fade like mist, into the flower-beds and
shrubbery. The old lady stood alone,
holding out her hands and looking up at
the fence between the two gardens.
"Blue! Blue, please come!"

Simon looked where she was looking, towards the fence, and thought for a moment that he saw, balancing there but walking away, a large, smoke-grey, plume-tailed cat, faint as a shadow in the last few moments before the sun goes in.

"Blue!" The old lady's voice sounded despairing now. The cat disappeared into the hollies at the end of the garden, and the old lady turned towards the house.

Simon couldn't see her any more, and by the time he woke up later in the morning he thought he had dreamed the whole thing.

But next night the smoke cat came back by itself. It was a moonlit night, and when Simon was in his room getting ready for bed he glanced out of the window, just in case. There was no old lady, no voice calling, but on the fence Simon could see the smoke cat, treading softly towards the house, balancing on

delicate paws. The cat paused, looked down into next-door's garden, rubbed itself against a fence post as cats do, and then turned and walked off slowly, stopping to look back. Simon couldn't help thinking that it looked disappointed.

"Blue! Come back!" Simon had opened the window and was shouting out before he knew why. The cat paused and looked up at him for a moment, wafting its plume of a tail. Then it walked off, along the fence, towards the hollies, where it faded and vanished like smoke melting into the air. Watching the place where it had gone, Simon felt an ache of loneliness, although he didn't know why. There was nothing there at all to show that Blue had ever been.

## Chapter 4

Two days later, Simon's mum had a dentist's appointment, and she told Simon that she wouldn't be in when he got back from school. "Hazel says you can go round to her house till I get home," she told him, "and she'll get you some tea."

Hazel seemed to be the sort of person who liked sticky cakes for tea, so Simon

didn't mind that at all. It was hot and
sunny on Thursday afternoon, and
Hazel came in from weeding the back
garden when he arrived. She stopped to
fetch Coke and jam doughnuts from the
kitchen (Simon wasn't disappointed)
and then they both went outside.

The garden looked a bit messier than Simon remembered it, although there was a bucket and a big pile of pulled weeds where Hazel had been working. He looked round, thinking that he knew some of these plants by name: Charlotte, Frederick, Gloria, William. But it would have sounded silly to say so. He wondered whether Hazel knew their names too.

"Did you plant all these flowers?" he asked her.

Hazel laughed. "Goodness, no." She snipped a dead flower from one of William's branches. "It takes a long time to get a garden looking like this. I just tidy it up now and then. No, my mother did most of the planting."

That explained it, although he still didn't know why Hazel hadn't told him her mother lived there, when he'd asked her the other day. Perhaps she was upstairs having a lie down. Old people did that, sometimes.

"Where is she?" he asked.

Hazel looked surprised. "My mum? Oh, she's dead now. She died two years ago."

Simon nearly said, "But she can't have done. I've seen her," until he realized that this was impossible; and besides, Hazel ought to know. He didn't *know*

what to say. He looked towards the house as if Hazel's mother might come out of the shadows. But there was no one there.

"Does – I mean did – your mother like cats?" he asked Hazel.

Hazel gave him a look of astonishment. "Yes! She was dotty about them. How did you guess?"

"Er – I just wondered." Simon was beginning to feel a bit peculiar. He eyed the third doughnut which was sitting by itself on the plate and wondered whether Hazel would mind if he had it. It would be a relief to eat another doughnut.

Doughnuts were solid and real, unlike old ladies who called to their cats in the middle of the night.

"Yes, she had dozens of cats over the years," Hazel said, looking towards Charlotte and not noticing how longingly

Simon was staring at the doughnut. "Four or five at a time. Of course they died sometimes, usually of old age. Whenever that happened she'd go to the garden centre and buy a new shrub and plant it, in memory – so nearly every plant in the garden's got a cat attached to it, if you see what I mean." Hazel gave a little laugh, as if she thought Simon might find this silly. "She even gave the plants names. Gloria, I remember. . . Frederick. . . I can't remember half of them now.

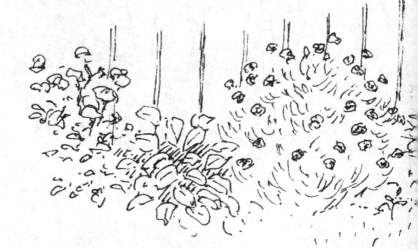

204

Simon wondered what she would say if he added, "Well, there's Charlotte, and there's Geoffrey. . ." But he didn't say anything. He was wondering about Blue. Why wouldn't Blue come into the garden, like the others? What did Blue want?

"She had a lovely cat just before she died," Hazel said. "A long-haired fluffy cat – grey, or more like blue-grey. She called him Blue."

"Yes, I know. I've seen him." This time the words were out of Simon's mouth before he could stop them.

Hazel stared at him.

"No, you can't have done," she said. "Blue died, a few weeks after Mum did. He wasn't very old. I don't know if a cat can pine, but I'm sure Blue pined for her."

She frowned. "Maybe there's another cat around that looks a bit like Blue. But he was an unusual cat, not the sort you see very often."

*No, it was definitely Blue.* Simon didn't say it, but he thought it. And then, like a whisper, he saw the smoke cat, a shadowy, furry shape creeping out from the deep shade of the hollies and wafting along the fence like a curl of smoke.

"There he is!" Simon shouted, before he could stop himself.

Hazel whipped round and looked straight at Blue, who paused, one paw lifted, and stared back. Then Hazel turned back to Simon, half-smiling, half-puzzled.

"There's nothing there. You're having a game with me."

"I'm not! He *is* there! Look!"

Just as before, Blue walked along the fence, hesitated as if about to jump down into the garden and then stopped. His mouth opened in a silent miaow and he curled himself around on the spot and

turned away. Just as before, Simon had the sense that Blue was disappointed. With a lash of his plume tail, Blue walked carefully along the fence towards the deep shade of the hollies. Simon's eyes followed the blurry shape until he was unsure whether it had ever been there. Hazel had got tired of the joke she thought he was playing, and had gone back to her weeding, not noticing.

Just then Mum arrived from the dentist's, with her mouth all lopsided from the injection she'd had. "Come on, Shimon," she said, keeping her mouth shut as tight as a ventriloquist's. "It'sh time to go home. Thanksh for having him, Hashel."

Indoors, Simon ran up to his room and looked out of the window, thinking about the things Hazel had said. It was obvious

that she hadn't seen or heard the old lady, nor did she see the smoke cat on the fence. As far as he could tell, he was the only person who saw them. It gave him the odd feeling that he was supposed to do something about it. Blue wanted something, and Simon sensed he was the only person who could try to guess what it was.

## Chapter 5

In the days and nights that followed, the old lady and the cat came back several times. There was no pattern to it. Sometimes, when he heard the old lady calling, it would be the middle of the night. Sometimes it would be broad sunlight, and she would be standing there in the garden for anyone to see, if only anyone else *could* see. Once, when Simon was watching from the apple tree, Hazel's husband Bill walked within inches of her without noticing.

Sometimes the old lady would be on her own, talking to her plants; sometimes she would be surrounded by her purring carpet of cats. But always she would be calling for Blue, and always Blue would turn away, disappointed. The old lady and Blue became so much a part of Simon's thoughts that he didn't know whether he dreamed them or really saw them. He only knew that he had to help them in some way – that he was the only person who *could*.

One afternoon, in desperation, he chased Blue right down the garden. It was useless; he should have known it would be. All that happened was that Blue vanished like a wisp of smoke into the evergreen depths of the hollies, and Simon plunged through the bushes on his own side of the fence, shouting, "Blue! Blue! Wait!" Even while he was

shouting he knew that the smoke cat
wouldn't wait; and he didn't even know
what he would have done if somehow he
had caught Blue. You can't catch and
keep a ghost cat; you can't make it stay.

At the end of the chase Simon found himself standing hopelessly in the thickest and thorniest bushes, with his face scratched, his sweatshirt snagged and his knees and hands grazed and stung. Blue was nowhere to be seen.

Mum stared at him when he went indoors. "What on earth have you been doing?" She didn't sound too pleased. "You look as if you've been dragged through a hedge backwards."

Forwards rather than backwards, but otherwise fairly true, Simon thought. It was too difficult to explain; who would believe him? "Just playing in the garden," he said off-handedly.

"Well, I wish you'd put something old on first," Mum said, still a bit cross. "That sweatshirt used to be quite smart." She was collecting her things together: purse, bag, cheque-book. "Do you want to come and help me choose a present for Hazel? It's her birthday on Sunday and she's invited us round."

"Where are you going to get it?"

Simon asked suspiciously. He didn't fancy trailing round perfume counters or looking at lacy scarves.

"I thought I'd go to the garden centre," Mum said. "Hazel's so keen on gardening – always out there digging and planting."

Simon wasn't sure why he agreed to go – garden centres weren't the most exciting places – but nevertheless he did. The garden centre was a huge place, with garden chairs and tools inside, and long avenues outside stretching into the distance, labelled *Climbers* or *Herbaceous Perennials*.

Mum started looking at hanging baskets bursting with pink geraniums and purple petunias, but Simon's attention was caught by the rows of bigger plants, all carefully looked after in their peaty-smelling containers, supported by sticks and labelled with their names. He looked at some, but they were in Latin and didn't

mean much to him. He found himself thinking, There's a Charlotte, and, That rose over there's a bit like William. And then it occurred to him. Blue didn't *have* a plant like the other cats, because the old lady had died first and hadn't been able to get him one. All the other cats came home to their own plant, but Blue always went away disappointed.

Here's my chance! Simon thought. I'll have to make Mum buy a Blue plant.

He walked along the rows, looking for a plant that would suit the smoke cat. There was row after row of yellow-flowered shrubs, pink-flowered climbers, scarlet perennials, some plants with no flowers at all. Nothing that would do. His spirits sank with dismay. If he didn't find the right plant here, where could he find it?

And then, turning a corner, he saw it at the end of a row ahead of him. It was so obviously the right plant for Blue that it seemed to call out to him. It had clusters of flowers like puffs of blue smoke, floating in a haze against darker leaves. He bent down as if greeting it, stroked the leaves, and then turned over

the label and read it. *Ceanothus Cerulea.*
A smoke plant for the smoke cat.

He tracked down Mum, who was
looking at some garish marigolds, and
said, "I've found it! Just what Hazel
wants."

"I was thinking perhaps a nice planted
arrangement. . ."

"No. This is what she wants!" Simon dragged her by the hand to where *Ceanothus Cerulea* was waiting. Mum was still looking back longingly at the brassy marigolds, but in the end she gave in and got out her cheque-book and Simon carried *Ceanothus Cerulea* to the counter inside.

## Chapter 6

Next day, at Hazel's, Simon couldn't wait until after the birthday tea for *Ceanothus Cerulea* to be planted. The garden table was loaded with all sorts of delicious things, and Hazel's husband Bill had made her a special cake with candles on it. Usually Simon's stomach would have started gurgling with delight, but not today – not yet. Blue's plant must come first.

"But I haven't decided where to put it yet," Hazel said, laughing. She was wearing new earrings and a new striped T-shirt and looked younger, not older, than she had done yesterday.

"I'll help you," Simon said. He dragged her towards the island bed and pointed. "Look, there. Just between Charlotte and Gloria. Blue's going to get quite big, so he'll need a bit of space."

Hazel stared at him. "Blue?"

"Yes. *You know.*" He looked at Hazel hard, meaning *Don't say anything to Mum and Dad – they won't understand.* He wasn't sure whether Hazel understood, but she looked at him oddly for a bit longer, then nodded and went and fetched a spade and a bag of bedding

compost. Simon helped with some of the digging – the ground was hard and dry – and when the hole was big enough,

Hazel's expert fingers arranged the earth around *Ceanothus Cerulea*'s roots as if she were tucking it into bed. Soon the new plant was firmly in its place, looking quite at home – cosily nestling between its two larger neighbours, but with plenty of room to grow.

"Now can we have our tea?" Simon's dad said, looking hungrily at the iced cake. "I had no idea you were so keen on gardening, Simon. There's plenty for you to do to our own jungle, if you want to get cracking. There's weeding and mowing and pruning and—"

"Not gardening," Simon said hastily. "Just this one plant."

He had done the best he could, but now he wanted to know that it had worked. When Hazel had blown out her forty candles and the cake had been cut and most of it eaten, Simon and his

parents went home. A little later, when the daylight started to fade, Simon went up to his room and looked out.

Nothing was happening. The garden table was still there, four garden chairs around it; Hazel's spade and compost-bag were beside the island bed where she had left them. There was no old lady, no smoke cat.

"Oh, come on, Blue!" Simon whispered, his mouth against the window. "I haven't gone to all this trouble for *nothing* – you must come now. . ."

Obstinately, the shadows refused to quiver into life and resolve themselves into the shape of a smoke cat. There was just a bare fence, and the hollies.

And then he heard, very faintly, "Charlotte, come along! William, there's a good boy! Gloria, where have you been?"

He craned his neck as far as he could. There she was, Hazel's mother, in her baggy cardigan and her droopy skirt, walking out from the patio into the dusk. The dim light streamed with furry shapes, surging, leaping down on to the grass, twining, tails high. The old lady walked

as far as the island bed and then she saw
*Ceanothus Cerulea.* She paused, and
stretched out a hand to touch it as if she
wasn't sure it was really there. Simon
hardly dared breathe. The shadows by
the hollies quivered and shook
themselves into the shadowy shape of a
cat. Blue. He sat, paused, and then
trotted along the fence with his plume
tail held high.

"Blue! Blue, come down!" The old
lady's voice was hopeful, not despairing.
Blue hesitated, opened his wide mouth
once in a silent miaow, and then bounded
down into the garden, where his shadowy
shape merged with the other cats. Hazel's

mother bent down to stroke him, and then the smoke cat took one joyful leap and landed lightly on her shoulders, twining himself around her ears. Just for a second, Simon thought the old lady looked up towards his window, and he saw her fleeting smile. The whole garden was filled with purring.

And then Simon blinked, and there was nothing there at all; just the silent gardens, and a rising moon.

The End